Dreena Hair

Written by Jan Burchett
and Sara Vogler

Illustrated by Monica Auriemma

Collins

Brook has black hair in long braids.
Scooter has short blond hair that
sticks up.

I am Scarlet. My long brown hair is down to my waist. Dreena is my twin. Dreena had long brown hair too.

But Dreena has been ill. She has lost her hair.

"I expect it will come back soon," says Mum.

Brook and Scooter paint cards
for Dreena.

"We are there for you," they tell her.

"Next week I will bring my dressing-up things," Scooter says.

And then we do dress up in Scooter's hats and crowns. Scooter hands Dreena a bright green scarf.

Brook twists the scarf into a crown and sticks flowers in it.

Brook slips it on Dreena. Dreena twists and turns. We clap.

"I look cool," Dreena tells us. "But I wish I had hair."

I plan to get my hairdresser to cut off my long brown hair. Then, my mum sends the hair to a trust.

The trust turns hair that is sent to them into wigs for children like Dreena.

They send a smart wig for Dreena, too.

Dreena loves it! Now she looks just like me!

Brook and Scooter bring books
for Dreena.

"Look!" says Dreena, pointing under
the wig.

Dreena has short brown hairs!

"Yippee!" we yell. We clap and jump in the air.

Dreena's hair

❧ Review: After reading ❧

Use your assessment from hearing the children read to choose any GPCs, words or tricky words that need additional practice.

Read 1: Decoding

- Read page 5, and point to the word **there**. Discuss its meaning in the phrase **there for you**, and how it doesn't mean a specific place but that they will help Dreena and support her.

- Practise sounding out words with adjacent consonants. Ask the children to read these words:

  brown   **bring**   **braids**   **waist**   **Scarlet**   **scarf**

  o   Let the children take turns to point to other words with adjacent consonants for a partner to read.

- Encourage the children to take turns to read a sentence. Encourage them to read fluently by saying: Try to sound out words in your head silently, as you read your sentence.

Read 2: Prosody

- Turn to pages 4 and 5. Ask the children to read the pages in groups of three, one taking the narrator's part, one reading Mum's spoken words, and another Brook's and Scooter's.

- Discuss how the characters are feeling and what tone they would use.

- Encourage groups to read the pages to the group.

Read 3: Comprehension

- Turn to page 4, and ask the children how they would feel if an illness affected their hair. Support children who may have experienced an illness leading to hair loss.

- Discuss why wigs help people like Dreena. Turn to page 11, and ask: Why do you think Dreena loves her wig?

- Discuss the statement, "Acts of kindness are important in this story" by discussing the actions of Mum, Scarlet, Scooter and Brook. Refer to the different parts of the story on pages 14 and 15. Ask:

  o   What is Mum saying to Dreena? Why? (e.g. *that her hair will probably grow back; to make her feel happier*)

  o   Why does Scarlet decide to have her hair cut off? (e.g. *to show support for her sister and to help children like Dreena*)

  o   Invite the children to use the pictures to retell the story in their own words.